This belongs to:

Lena Salto

The Secret Garden

A DK Publishing Book
www.dk.com

Art Editor Tanya Tween
Senior Editor Marie Greenwood
Managing Art Editor Jacquie Gulliver
Picture Research Andrea Sadler and Cynthia Frazer
DTP Designer Jill Bunyan
Production Joanne Rooke

First American Edition, 1999

2 4 6 8 10 9 7 5 3 1

Published in the United States by
DK Publishing, Inc.
95 Madison Avenue
New York, New York 10016

McKellar, Shona.
   The secret garden/by Frances Hodgson Burnett; adapted by
Shona McKellar; illustrated by Tony Kerins. --1st American ed.
   p.   cm. -- (Young classics)
Summary: An abbreviated version of the classic story of the ten-
year-old orphan who goes to live in a lonely house on the
Yorkshire moors where she discovers an invalid cousin and the
mysteries of a locked garden.
   ISNB 0-7894-4943-9
   [1. Orphans Fiction. 2. Gardens Fiction. 3. Physically
handicapped Fiction. 4. Yorkshire (England) Fiction.
5. England Fiction.] I Burnett, Frances Hodgson, 1849–1924, Secret
Garden. II Kerins, Tony, ill, III. Title. IV. Series.
PZ7. M478673Se   1999
[Fic]--dc21
                                 99-33392
                                   CIP

Color reproduction by Bright Arts, Hong Kong
Printed in Italy by L.E.G.O.

Acknowledgments

The publisher would like to thank the following for their kind permission to reproduce their photographs:

a=above; c=center; b=bottom/below; l=left; r=right; t=top
Tony Barton Collection: 23br; **Bridgeman Art Library, London/New York:** 14 tl; **Christie's Images Ltd:** 1999 Sir Joshua Reynolds 6 bc;
Colorific: Richard Passmore 9 tr; **Mary Evans Picture Library:** 10 cr, 48 cl, 48 clb; **Ronald Grant Archive:** 1993 by Warner Bros: 46 clb;
Hulton Getty: 48 cr; **Huntington Library:** inside jacket flap, 48 tl; **Andrew Lawson:** 45 cra, Barnsley House, Glos. 45 tc; **Marianne Majerus:** 48 br;
National Trust Photographic Library: Andrew Lawson 44 cl, Neil Campbell-Sharp 47 tr; **Clive Nichols:** Wollerton Old Hall, Shropshire 46 cra;
Pictor International: 47 cl; **Harry Smith Collection:** 44 bl.

The publisher would particularly like to thank the following people:
Alastair Dougall and Jacky Jackson (editorial assistance); Chris Molan (additional illustration); Laia Roses
and Lisa Lanzerini (design assistance).

YOUNG **DK** CLASSICS

The Secret Garden

By **Frances Hodgson Burnett**
Adapted by **Shona McKellar**

DK
DK Publishing, Inc.

Illustrated by
Tony Kerins

Contents

✳

✳

Mistress Mary

EVERYBODY SAID that Mary Lennox was the most disagreeable-looking child ever seen. She had a little thin face and a little thin body, thin light hair, and a sour expression. Her hair was yellow, and her face was yellow because she had lived in India and had often been sick.

Mary's father was always busy working or else he was ill himself, and her mother was a great beauty who liked to go to lots of parties. They didn't want to be disturbed by their daughter so they handed her over to the care of an *ayah*. Her *ayah* always did what Mary wanted, as she knew her mother would be angry if she was disturbed by Mary crying. This had made her into a very selfish child who was used to getting her own way.

One particular morning there was something mysterious in the air. Nothing was done in its regular order and several of the servants seemed to be missing. But no one would tell Mary anything.

Suddenly a loud wailing broke out from the servants' quarters. A terrible illness, cholera, had broken out, and people were dying. In all the confusion Mary was forgotten by everyone. Nobody thought of her, nobody wanted her, and strange things happened of which she knew nothing.

When Mary woke the next day, the house was quite still. It was as if she was all alone. Then she heard footsteps.

Mary was standing in the middle of the nursery when two

In the early 1900s, when this story begins, India was under British rule, and many British families had settled there. Mary has been brought up by her ayah, *an Indian nanny.*

officers opened
the door. She looked
an ugly, angry little thing
and was frowning.

One officer was so startled that
he jumped back. "There is a child
here! A child alone!"

It was in this strange and sudden
way that Mary found out that both
her parents had died of cholera.
All the servants had died or fled.
It was true that she was all alone.

Soon after, Mary was told she was
to travel to England – to live with her
uncle, Mr. Archibald Craven, who lived at
Misselthwaite Manor on the edge of the
Yorkshire moors.

*"There is a child here!
A child alone!"*

Mrs. Medlock and Mary made a strange pair.

The train rattled and shook from side to side. Mary looked out of the window at the passing countryside, a glum expression on her face. Mrs. Medlock, the housekeeper at Misselthwaite Manor, stared at Mary Lennox and thought what a plain child she was. In contrast, Mrs. Medlock was stout, with red cheeks and sharp, black eyes. They made a strange pair. Mrs. Medlock had met Mary in London, and now they were traveling up to Yorkshire together.

Mrs. Medlock broke the uncomfortable silence. "I suppose you might as well be told something to prepare you. Misselthwaite Manor is an odd place. It's a big, grand house with about one hundred rooms, though most of them are shut up. Your uncle, Mr. Archibald Craven, is proud of it in his way. The house is on the edge of the moor in Yorkshire and is nearly six hundred years old."

The journey through the wild, bleak Yorkshire moors in northern England can only add to Mary's feelings of loneliness.

Mary had begun to listen in spite of herself. It all sounded so unlike India.

"Now don't expect Mr. Craven to take an interest in you," said Mrs. Medlock. "Most of the time he is away. He doesn't want to stay at Misselthwaite since his wife died. She was a sweet, pretty thing, and he would have walked the world over to get her a blade of grass. Nobody thought she would marry him, as he has a crooked back, but she did. Since her death Mr. Craven cares about nobody." Mary thought everything sounded so strange, like something

out of a book. "You'll have your own rooms," continued Mrs. Medlock, "and you are not to go poking about into any others. There's plenty of garden to play in, though."

Mary stared out of the window at the rain streaming down and felt cold and miserable. Slowly she felt her eyes closing and fell asleep.

She awoke at the station. After a long drive across the moor, they finally reached the house and went into an enormous hall. As Mary stood on the stone floor she looked a small, odd little figure, and she felt as small and lost and odd as she looked.

"I don't like it," she said to herself. "I don't like it," and she pinched her thin lips more tightly together. ✳

Misselthwaite Manor

WHEN MARY OPENED HER EYES in the morning it was because a young housemaid had come into her room to light the fire.

"Are you going to be my servant?" Mary demanded.

"I'm Mrs. Medlock's servant," replied Martha stoutly, "but I'm to do the housemaid's work up here and wait on you a bit."

Mary looked out of the window at a great treeless stretch of land which looked like an endless, purplish sea.

"What is that?"

"That's the moor," said Martha, cheerfully polishing away at the grate. "I just love it. It's covered with growing things that smell sweet. It looks lovely in spring and summer when the gorse and broom and heather are in flower. It smells of honey, and the skylarks make a beautiful noise with their singing."

As a housemaid, Martha has many duties to attend to, and has no time to wait on Mary hand and foot. She speaks to Mary as an equal – something Mary is not used to.

Mary looked at Martha in surprise. The servants in India had never talked to her like that.

"Are you going to dress me?" she demanded rudely.

Martha sat back on her heels and stared at Mary in amazement.

"Can't you dress yourself?"

"No," answered Mary, quite coldly. "I never have in my life."

Mary stood still as though she had neither hands nor feet of her own and waited for the housemaid to dress her. Martha showed Mary how to put on her shoes and stockings and chatted about her family. "There's twelve of us altogether. All my brothers and sisters play out on the moor all day and my mother says the air fattens them up. Dickon, my brother who is twelve, has got a pony he found on the moor. He's wonderful with animals, is Dickon."

Martha brought in a good breakfast, but Mary had always had a small appetite and was not interested. She pecked at some toast.

"You wrap up warm and run out and play," said Martha. "It will do you good and give you an appetite."

"Who will come with me?"

"You'll have to learn to play on your own. Our Dickon goes off on the moor and plays with the animals for hours."

Martha pointed out the gardens from the window. "One of the gardens is locked up. No one has been in it for ten years."

Mary could not help being interested. "Why?" she demanded.

"Mr. Craven had it shut up when his wife died as it was her garden. He won't let anyone go inside. He has locked the door and buried the key. There's Mrs. Medlock's bell ringing – I must run!"

"Are you going to dress me?"

Mary went out into the gardens. There were trees, flowerbeds, and evergreens clipped into strange shapes, and a large pool with an old gray fountain in the middle. She came to a long wall with ivy growing over it. An open door led into a kitchen garden where an old man was digging. He looked startled when he saw Mary and then touched his cap, but he did not seem at all pleased to see her.

Mary could see the tops of the trees above the wall and on one of these sat a robin. Suddenly he burst into song – almost as if he was calling to her. Mary stopped and listened, and somehow his cheerful song gave her a happy feeling. To her surprise the old man began to smile; then he gave a low, soft whistle. There was a rushing flight through the air and the robin landed by the gardener's foot.

"Will he always come when you call him?" she whispered.

"Yes, he will. I've known him since he was young. He came out of the nest in the other garden, and he was too weak to fly back over the wall. He was lonely and we became friends."

"I'm lonely," said Mary.

Mary went a step nearer to the robin and looked at him very hard.

Mary wanders through several walled kitchen gardens where all kinds of fruit and vegetables are grown — but one garden she cannot enter.

"I'm lonely," she said.

She had not known before that this was one of the things which made her feel unhappy and angry. She seemed to find it out when the robin looked at her and she looked at the robin.

Mary turned to the old man. "What is your name?"

"Ben Weatherstaff," he answered, and then added with a surly chuckle, "I'm lonely myself except when he's with me," and he jerked his thumb toward the robin. "He's the only friend I've got."

"I have no friends at all," said Mary. "I never have."

"Then you and me are a good bit alike," said Ben. "We're neither of us good-looking, and we are both as sour as we look."

This was plain speaking. Mary Lennox had never heard the truth about herself before, and it made her feel uncomfortable.

Suddenly the robin burst into song.

"Would you make friends with me?" said Mary to the robin, just as if she were speaking to a person. "Would you?"

The robin gave a little shake of his wings and then flew away. "He has flown over the wall!" Mary cried out, watching him. "Now he has flown across the other wall — into the garden with no door!"

"He lives there," said old Ben, "among the old rose trees."

"Rose trees," said Mary. "Are there rose trees?"

Ben Weatherstaff took up his spade again and began to dig.

"There was ten years ago," he mumbled.

"I should like to see them," said Mary. "Where is the door? There must be one somewhere."

"Not that anyone can find. Now don't be a meddlesome child and go poking your nose into things that don't concern you." He stopped digging, threw his spade over his shoulder, and walked off without even glancing at her or saying goodbye.

Mary believes that Misselthwaite Manor, with its maze of dark passageways and tapestry-covered walls, conceals a secret.

Mary went out into the gardens almost every day. She did not realize, as she ran along the paths and breathed in the fresh moorland air, that she was making herself healthier and stronger.

One wild and wet day, Mary had to stay indoors with Martha. As they sat listening to the wind whistling around the house, Mary became aware of another noise. It was a curious sound – it seemed almost as if a child were crying somewhere.

"Do you hear anyone crying?" asked Mary.

Martha suddenly looked confused. "No. It's just the wind."

But something troubled in her manner made Mary stare very hard at Martha – she did not believe she was telling the truth.

Later that day, Mary decided to explore the house. As she wandered around upstairs and down, through narrow passages and from room to room, she felt as if there was no one in all the huge, rambling house but her own small self. Most of the doors were locked, but a few of them opened. The rooms were furnished but there was no sign of life, except in one, where Mary found a family of mice which had made a nest in a cushion.

She was trying to find the way back to her own room when the stillness was broken by a sound. "It's nearer than it was," said Mary, her heart beating rather faster. "And it *is* crying."

She accidentally put her hand on a hanging tapestry near her, and then sprang back. The tapestry covered a door which fell open and showed her another part of the corridor behind it. Mrs. Medlock was coming along with a bunch of keys in her hand and a very angry look on her face.

"What are you doing here?" she asked angrily.

"I came down the wrong corridor, I didn't know which way to go and I heard someone crying."

Mrs. Medlock was coming along with an angry look on her face.

"You didn't hear anything of the sort," said the housekeeper. "You come along back to your own nursery or I'll box your ears."

And she took Mary by the arm and half pushed, half pulled her back to the door of her own room. Mary went and sat on the hearthrug, pale with rage.

"There *was* someone crying – there *was* – there *was*!" she said to herself. ✽

The Key to the Garden

Martha had the day off and was going to visit her family. It was a five-mile walk across the moor to her cottage. Mary felt lonelier than ever when she knew Martha wasn't in the house, so she went out into the garden as quickly as possible.

She soon found Ben Weatherstaff working in the kitchen garden. The sunny weather seemed to have done him good and he spoke to her in a friendly way. "Springtime's coming," he said.

They talked for a little, and then Mary heard the soft rustling of

Robins are bold birds with little fear of humans, so they often appear friendly. Mary is not used to being noticed by anybody.

wings and she knew at once that the robin had come. She was so pleased to see it.

"Do you think he remembers me?" she asked.

"Remembers you!" said Ben indignantly. "He knows every cabbage stump in the gardens, let alone the people."

Mary felt lonelier than ever once Martha had gone.

Mary walked down to the long, ivy-covered wall over which she could see the treetops, and the robin came too. Mary heard a chirp and a twitter, and when she looked at the bare flowerbed there he was hopping around. Mary knew then that he had followed her, and the surprise so filled her with delight that she trembled a little.

"You do remember me!" she cried. "You do! You are prettier than anything else in the world!"

He hopped and flirted with his tail, and twittered. It was as if he were talking to her. Mary was so happy that she scarcely dared breathe.

She saw the robin hop over a small pile of freshly turned-up earth. He stopped to look for a worm. The earth had been turned up because a dog had scratched a deep hole.

Mary looked at it, not really knowing why the hole was there, and as she looked she saw something almost buried in the newly turned soil. It looked like a ring of rusty iron or brass. When she picked it up she realized it was more than a ring, though; it was an old key which looked as if it had been buried a long time.

Mary stood up and looked at it with an almost frightened face as it hung from her finger.

"Perhaps it has been buried for ten years," she said in a whisper. "Perhaps it is the key to the garden!"

It was an old key which had been buried a long time.

Martha returned from her visit to her family full of stories of the delights of her day out. She brought with her a skipping rope as a present for Mary from her mother. Martha's mother felt sorry for Mary, although with fourteen people in her family she didn't really have any spare money for buying presents.

Mary Lennox had never seen a skipping rope before. She gazed at it with a puzzled expression.

"What is it for?" she asked curiously.

"For!" cried Martha. "This is what it's for; just watch me."

Taking a handle in each hand, Martha began to skip, while Mary turned in her chair to stare at her.

"Do you think I could ever skip like that?" asked Mary.

"You just try it," urged Martha, handing her the skipping rope.

Mary turned to Martha and said "thank you" rather stiffly. She was not used to thanking people or noticing when they did things for her.

The skipping rope was a wonderful thing. Mary skipped all around the gardens until her cheeks were quite red. After some time, she went to her own special walk which she loved to run along, and made up her mind to see if she could skip the whole length of it. But before she had skipped halfway down the path she was so hot and breathless she had to stop.

Then Mary saw the robin. He greeted her with a chirp and she laughed. "You showed me where the key was before," she said. "You ought to show me the door today; but I don't believe you know!"

Mary Lennox had heard a great deal about magic in her *ayah's* stories, and she always said that what happened next was magic. A gust of wind rushed down the walk, swaying the trailing sprays of untrimmed ivy hanging from the wall. Mary suddenly noticed a round knob in the wall that

Mary holds the key to the secret garden and the key to her own private world.

had previously been covered by the leaves. It was the knob of a door.

Her heart began to thump and her hands to shake a little in her excitement. The robin kept singing and twittering away and tilting his head on one side, as if he were as excited as she was.

Her fingers found the lock of the door. She pulled the key from her pocket and turned the lock.

Then Mary took a long breath and looked behind her up the long walk to make sure no one was coming. She pushed back the door which opened slowly – slowly.

Mary slipped through the door and shut it behind her. She stood looking about – breathing quite fast with excitement, and wonder, and delight.

She was standing *inside* the secret garden.

Mary looked behind her to make sure no one was coming.

It was the sweetest, most mysterious-looking place anyone could imagine. The high walls which shut it in were covered with the leafless stems of climbing roses. Mary did not know whether they were dead or alive, but their thin gray or brown branches and sprays looked like a sort of hazy web spreading over everything. It was this tangle from tree to tree which made it look so mysterious.

"How still it is!" she whispered. "How still. I am the first person who has spoken in here for ten years." She walked under one of the fairylike arches between the trees and looked up.

"Is it all a dead garden? I wish it wasn't." But she was inside the wonderful garden, and she could come through the door under the ivy any time, and she felt as if she had found a world all her own.

Mary thought she saw something sticking out of the black earth – some sharp, little, pale green points. "They are tiny growing things – they might be crocuses or snowdrops or daffodils," she whispered. "It isn't a dead garden. Even if the roses are dead, there are other things alive."

She did not know anything about gardening, but the grass seemed so thick in some of the places where the green points were pushing their way through that she thought they did not seem to

have room enough to grow.
She searched about until she found
a sharp piece of wood and knelt down
and dug and weeded out the weeds and grass until
she made nice little clear places around them.

"Now they look as if they could breathe,"
she said, after she had finished with the first ones.
"I am going to do ever so many more. I'll do all I can
see. If I haven't time today I can come tomorrow."

Mary worked in her garden until it was time to go
for lunch. While Mary ate she talked to Martha.
"Martha, I would like to have a little garden.
How much would a spade cost – a little one?"

"At Thwaite village there is a shop with little
garden sets for two shillings. They also sell packets
of flowers for a penny each. Our Dickon often walks
over to Thwaite just for fun. If you could print we
could send a letter to Dickon and ask him to go
and buy the things for you."

So Mary printed the letter and put the
money in an envelope for the butcher's
boy to give to Dickon.

"How shall I get the things
when Dickon buys them?"
asked Mary.

"He'll bring them to you himself."
"Oh!" exclaimed Mary, "then I shall
see him! I never saw a boy foxes and crows
loved! I want to see him very much."

The sun shone down for nearly a week on the secret garden. The secret garden was what Mary called it when she was thinking of it. She liked the name, and she liked still more the feeling that when its beautiful old walls shut her in, no one knew where she was. Mary worked and dug and pulled up weeds steadily, only becoming more pleased with her work every hour instead of tiring of it.

One day she was skipping in the garden when she thought she would go into the wood. There she saw a boy sitting with his back against a tree playing on a wooden pipe. He was a funny-looking boy of about twelve. He looked very clean, and his nose turned up and his cheeks were as red as poppies. Never had Mistress Mary seen such round and such blue eyes in any boy's face. He was surrounded by animals.

"I'm Dickon," the boy said. "I know that you are Miss Mary. I've got the garden tools. There's a little spade and rake and a fork and hoe.

Mary saw a boy playing
a wooden pipe.

"Eh! They are good ones. There's a trowel, too. And the woman in the shop threw in a packet of white poppies and one of blue larkspurs when I bought the other seeds."

"Will you show the seeds to me?" Mary said. "Let's sit down on this log and look at them."

Dickon told Mary what they looked like when y were flowers; he told her how to plant them, and watch n, and feed and water them.

'See here," he said suddenly. "I'll plant them for you myself. re is your garden?"

Iary did not know what to say at first. Then she turned her oward him. "Could you keep a secret? It's a great secret; t know what I should do if anyone found it out."

ckon looked very puzzled. "I'm keeping secrets all the he said. "If I couldn't keep secrets from the other lads, about foxes' cubs, and birds' d wild things' holes, there'd ing safe on the moor."

stolen a garden," Mary blurted out. "Nobody wants y cares for it, nobody ever it."

re is it?" asked Dickon very quietly.

e with me and I'll show you," she said.

n Mary stepped up to the wall and lifted the hanging ivy Dickon started in surprise. Mary pushed the door slowly open and they passed in together.

Dickon is in tune with nature and charms animals by playing a pipe, like Pan, the ancient Greek god of nature.

For two or three minutes Dickon stood looking around him. "It's a strange, pretty place," he whispered. "It's as if a body were in a dream." His eyes seemed to be taking in everything – the gray trees with the gray creepers climbing over them and hanging from their branches, the tangle on the wall and among the grass, the evergreen alcoves with the stone seats and tall flower urns standing in them.

"Will there be roses?" Mary whispered. "Can you tell? I thought perhaps they were all dead."

"Not all of them," he answered.

"Look here!" He stepped over to a curtain of tangled sprays and branches. "They've run wild," he said, "but the strongest ones have grown and spread. With care from us, there'll be a fountain of roses here this summer."

They went from tree to tree and from bush to bush. Dickon knew how to cut the dry, dead wood away, and could tell when an unpromising bough or twig still had green life in it. Soon, Mary thought she could tell too, and when he cut through a lifeless-looking branch she would cry out joyfully if she saw the least shade of moist green. They were working around one of the biggest rose bushes when Dickon caught sight of something.

"Why!" he cried. "Who did that?"

It was one of Mary's clearings.

By clearing a space in the garden, Mary has helped the crocuses and snowdrops to grow. These flowers are a sign that spring is on its way.

"I did," said Mary.

"I thought you knew nothing about gardening!"

"I don't, but they were so little and the grass was so thick and strong, and they looked as if they had no room to breathe. I don't even know what they are."

Dickon knelt by them, smiling his wide smile. "You were right. A gardener couldn't have told you better. Now they'll grow like Jack's beanstalk. They're crocuses and snowdrops, and these are daffodils. You have done a lot of work."

"I always used to be tired, but when I dig I'm not tired at all."

"There's a lot of work to do!" Dickon said looking around.

"Will you come again and help me to do it?" Mary begged. "Oh! do come, Dickon!"

"I'll come every day if you want me, rain or shine," he answered. "It's the best fun I ever had in my life – shut in here and wakening up a garden."

"A gardener couldn't have told you better," said Dickon.

Mary ran back so fast from the garden that she was out of breath when she reached her room. Her hair was ruffled and her cheeks were bright pink. Mary's dinner was waiting on the table.

"You're a bit late," said Martha. "Where have you been?"

Mary excitedly told her how she had met Dickon. After hurriedly finishing her food, she was about to dash outdoors again before Martha stopped her.

"I've got something to tell you," she said. "Mr. Craven came back this morning and I think he wants to see you."

"When do you think he will want to see – " Mary did not finish the sentence because the door opened, and Mrs. Medlock walked in.

"Your hair's rough," she said quickly. "Go and brush it. Martha, help her to slip on her best dress. Mr. Craven sent me to bring her to him in his study."

All the pink left Mary's cheeks. Her heart began to thump and she felt herself changing into a stiff, plain, silent child again. She knew she had to go and see Mr. Craven, and he would not like her, and she would not care for him. She knew what he would think of her.

Mary was taken to Mr. Craven's study. A man was sitting in an armchair before the fire. She could see he was not so much a hunchback as a man with high, rather crooked shoulders, and he had black hair streaked with white. He looked as if the sight of her worried him and as if he did not know what in the world to do with her.

"Are you well?" he asked.

"Yes," answered Mary.

"Do they take good care of you?"

"Yes."

"I intended to send you a governess or nurse or someone of that sort, but I forgot," said Mr. Craven.

"Please," began Mary, "I am too big for a nurse. And please don't make me have a governess yet."

"What do you want to do?"

"I want to play outdoors," Mary answered, hoping that her voice did not tremble.

"Mrs. Sowerby, Martha's mother, said it would do you good. Perhaps it will," he said. "Play outdoors as much as you like. Is there anything you want? Do you want toys, books, dolls?"

"Might I," Mary asked anxiously, "might I have a bit of earth?"

Mr. Craven looked quite startled. "Earth!" he repeated. "What do you mean?"

"To plant seeds in – to make things grow – to see them come alive," Mary said hesitantly.

"A bit of earth," he said to himself, and Mary thought that somehow she must have reminded him of something. When he stopped and spoke to her his dark eyes looked almost soft and kind.

"You can have as much earth as you want," he said. "When you see a bit of earth you want, take it, child, and make it come alive. There! You must go now, I am tired." He touched the bell to call Mrs. Medlock. "Goodbye. I shall be away all summer." ✽

"When you see a bit of earth you want, take it, and make it come alive!"

"I am Colin"

MARY HAD BEEN LYING AWAKE when something suddenly made her sit up in bed and turn her head toward the door.

"It isn't the wind," she thought. "It's the crying I heard before." Taking a candle from her bedside, she went softly out of the room. The corridor looked very long and dark, but she thought she remembered how to find the door covered with tapestry – the one Mrs. Medlock had come through. The far-off, faint crying went on and led her. At last she came to the tapestry door and, with beating heart, pushed it open.

There was a carved, four-poster bed, and lying on it was a boy, crying pitifully. He had a sharp, delicate face, the color of ivory, and his eyes seemed too big for his face.

Mary stood near the door with her candle in her hand, holding her breath.

"Who are you?" the boy said at last in a half-frightened whisper. "Are you a ghost?"

"No, I am not," Mary answered. "Are you one?"

"No," he replied. "I am Colin. Who are you?"

"I am Mary Lennox. Mr. Craven is my uncle."

"He is my father," said the boy.

"Your father!" gasped Mary. "No one ever told me he had a boy! Why didn't they?"

"Because I should have been afraid you would see me. I won't let people see me and talk about me. I am like this always, ill and having to lie down. If I live I may be a hunchback, but I shan't live. My father hates to think I may be like him."

"Does your father come and see you?"

"Sometimes. Generally when I am asleep. My mother died when I was born and it makes him wretched to look at me. He thinks

I don't know, but I've heard people talking. I'm looked after by Dr. Craven, my father's cousin. How old are you?" he asked suddenly.

"I am ten," answered Mary, "and so are you."

"How do you know that?" he demanded in a surprised voice.

"Because when you were born the garden door was locked and the key was buried. And it has been locked for ten years."

"What garden door was locked? Who did it? Where was the key buried?" he exclaimed, immediately interested. "I want to see that garden. I want the key dug up. I want the door unlocked."

Mary answered, almost with a sob in her throat, "But if you make them open the door it will never be a secret again."

"A secret?" he said. "What do you mean? Tell me."

Mary's words tumbled over one another as she explained.

"Perhaps," said Mary, "we could find some boy to push

*"Who are you?"
said the boy.*

you, and we could go alone; then it would always be a secret garden."

"I would – like – that," he said very slowly, his eyes looking dreamy. "I want you to come here and talk to me about the secret garden every day." Then his eyes shut and he fell fast asleep.

"I have got something to tell you," said Mary to Martha the following morning. "I now know what the crying was. It was Colin."

Martha's face became red with fright. "Miss Mary!" she cried.

"Don't worry, he is not going to tell Mrs. Medlock anything," said Mary. "He was glad I came, and it is to be our secret. He wants me to come and talk to him every day. And you are to tell me when he wants me. He says everybody is obliged to do as he pleases."

"You shouldn't have done it. I shall lose my job!"

"You can't if you are doing what he wants you to do and everybody is ordered to obey him," argued Mary.

Very soon afterward a bell rang, and Martha rolled up her knitting. "I dare say the nurse wants me to stay with Colin for a bit. I hope he is in a good temper."

She was out of the room for about ten minutes and then came back with a puzzled expression.

"You have bewitched him. He has sent me to fetch you."

There was a bright fire on the hearth when Mary entered his room. Colin was sat on a sofa, reading some picture books.

"Come in," he said. "I've been thinking about you all morning." Mary stood and silently gazed at the pale-faced boy.

"Why do you look at me like that?" he asked her. "What are you thinking about?"

"I was thinking," said Mary, "how different you are from Dickon."

"Who is Dickon?" he asked.

Mary told Colin all about Dickon – how he understood animals and growing things and how he loved the moor.

"Dickon is not like anyone else in the world," said Mary. "He would make you want to live."

They chatted for some time about Dickon and Martha and their little cottage on the moor, and they both began to laugh over nothing as children will when they are happy together. They enjoyed themselves so much they forgot about the time and were soon making as much noise as two ordinary, healthy, natural children. And in the middle of the fun the door opened and in walked Dr. Craven and Mrs. Medlock.

"Good Lord!" exclaimed Mrs. Medlock, her eyes almost starting out of her head.

"What does this mean?" said Dr. Craven, coming forward.

"This is my cousin, Mary Lennox," Colin said. "I asked her to come and talk to me. I like her. She must come and see me whenever I send for her. Mary makes me better. The nurse will bring up her tea with mine.

"They are always wanting me to eat things when I don't want to," said Colin. "But if you'll eat I will. Tell me about *rajahs*."

"Good Lord!" exclaimed Mrs. Medlock.

The next day, Mary woke up very early. The sky was blue, the sun was pouring in slanting rays through the blinds, and there was something so joyous in the sight of it that she jumped out of bed and ran to open the window. A great waft of fresh, scented air blew in upon her. The moor was blue and the whole world looked as if something magic had happened to it. Mary put her hand out of the window and held it in the sun.

"It's warm – warm!" she said. "It will make the bulbs and roots struggle with all their might under the earth and the green points push up and up and up. I can't wait! I'm going to see the garden."

She knew a small door she could unbolt to let herself out. Then she ran around the shrubs and paths toward the secret garden.

"It's so different already," she said. "The grass is greener and flowers are sticking up everywhere and things are uncurling and green buds of leaves are showing. This afternoon I am sure Dickon will come."

When Mary entered the secret garden she found Dickon already kneeling on the grass working hard.

They ran from one part of the garden to another and found many wonders.

"Oh, Dickon! Dickon!" she said. "I'm so happy I can scarcely breathe." They ran from one part of the garden to another and found so many wonders that they had to remind themselves that they must be quiet.

There was every joy on earth in the secret garden that morning, and then came the most delightful surprise of all. Swiftly something flew across the wall and darted through the trees to an overgrown corner. It was a red-breasted bird with something hanging from its beak.

"It's Ben Weatherstaff's robin," whispered Dickon. "He's building his nest. He'll stay here if we don't frighten him. But if we are too curious he will go somewhere else."

"I can't help looking at him," Mary said softly. "Dickon, there is something I want to tell you. Do you know about Colin?"

Spring has come and blossoms hang heavy on the trees. Just as the garden is waking up to new life, so is Mary growing and changing.

Dickon turned his head to look at her. "What do you know about him?" he asked.

"I have been to talk to him every day this week. He says I'm making him forget about being ill and dying," answered Mary.

Dickon looked relieved. "I'm glad about that. If Colin was out here with us he wouldn't be worrying about lumps growing on his back; he'd be too busy looking at all the things in the garden."

"He's been lying in his room so long, and he's always been so afraid of his back it has made him strange," said Mary. "Do you think you could push his chair?"

"Yes," said Dickon. "It would be so good for him to be outside in the garden."

"I can't stop!" Colin gasped and sobbed. "I can't!"

Mary thought it was the middle of the night when she was awakened by such dreadful sounds that she jumped out of bed in an instant. What was it?

The next minute she felt quite sure she knew. Doors were opened and shut and there were hurrying feet in the corridors and someone was crying and screaming at the same time.

"It's Colin," she thought. "He's having a tantrum. How awful it sounds!"

Just then she heard feet running down the corridor, her door opened and the nurse came in. "He'll do himself harm. No one can do anything with him. You come and try."

Mary rushed along the corridor, and the nearer she got to the screams the crosser she became. She ran into his room and stormed up to the four-poster bed. "You stop!" Mary shouted.

"I can't!" Colin gasped, and sobbed. "I felt the lump. I shall have a hunch on my back and then I shall die."

"Colin," commanded Mary, "show me your back this minute." Mary looked up and down his spine very carefully. "There's not a single lump there!" she said at last. "If you ever say there is again, I shall laugh!"

Colin was amazed by Mary's angry words. Nobody else had ever spoken to him like that. He felt that Mary might be speaking the truth about his back, and was beginning to realize that his fear and illness were created by one person – himself.

Like Mary, Colin has spent much of his time alone – but now with the help of Dickon and his animals, he is learning to make friends.

Mary and Colin were calm now and they settled down to talk by themselves. Mary told him all about the secret garden and that Dickon would take him there.

The next day Dickon arrived with his animals to see Colin. He came in smiling his nicest wide smile. A newborn lamb was in his arms and a little red fox trotted by his side. One squirrel sat on his left shoulder and a crow on his right and another squirrel peeped out of his coat pocket.

Colin slowly sat up and stared and stared. He had never talked to another boy in his life, and he was so delighted that he did not even think of speaking. But Dickon did not feel shy or awkward and walked over to Colin's sofa and put the lamb on his lap.

Soon all the children were chatting together. While they talked the crow flew in and out of the open window and Nut and Shell, the squirrels, ran up and down the big trees outside.

Together they looked at pictures of flowers in a book. Dickon knew all the flowers by their country names and which ones were already growing in the secret garden.

"I'm going to see them," cried Colin excitedly. "I'm going to see them!" ✳

Soon all the children were chatting together.

Magic in the Garden

THE CHILDREN HAD TO WAIT for more than a week to go out. Preparations had to be made before Colin could be taken with enough secrecy to the garden. No one must see how the children entered the secret garden. Colin now understood that the mystery surrounding the garden was one of its greatest charms.

The day for Colin's first outing finally came and the strongest servant in the house carried him downstairs and put him in his wheelchair. Colin grandly waved his hand to him.

"You may leave," he said.

Dickon began to push the wheelchair steadily down the garden paths. Mary walked beside it and Colin leaned back and lifted his face to the sky. Nobody else was to be seen. Eventually they reached the secret garden. Dickon pushed Colin's chair in with one strong push.

Looking around, Colin saw the splashes of color, heard the

"Look!" Colin whispered excitedly. "Just look!"

fluttering of wings, and smelled wonderful scents.
In wonder, Mary and Dickon stood and stared at him.
He looked so strange and different and a pink glow
of color had crept all over his ivory face.

"I shall get well!" he cried out.
"And I shall live forever!"

Delight reigned as they pushed the chair
slowly around and around the garden, stopping
every other moment to let Colin gaze at
wonders springing out of the earth or trailing
down from trees. The afternoon was full of new
things, and every hour the sunshine grew more golden.

Suddenly Colin exclaimed in a loud, alarmed whisper,
"Look! Just look! Who is that man?" Colin was pointing
to the high wall.

Dickon and Mary scrambled to their feet. There was Ben
Weatherstaff glaring at them over the wall from the top of a ladder!
They looked up at him in alarm. "Do you know who I am?"
demanded Colin. "Answer!"

The old man put his rough hand up to shade his eyes and then
he answered in a strange, shaking voice, "Of course I know who you
are — with your mother's eyes staring at me from out of your face.
You're the boy with crooked legs."

Colin forgot that he had ever had problems with his back.
His face flushed scarlet and he sat bolt upright. Never before had he
been accused of crooked legs. Anger and insulted pride filled him
with a power he had never known before, an almost unnatural strength.

Throwing off his blankets, Colin called to Dickon to hold his
arm and then the thin legs were out and the thin feet were on the
grass. Colin stood upright as straight as an arrow.

"Look at me!" he called out to Ben Weatherstaff. "Am I a
hunchback? Have I got crooked legs?"

The roses are in full bloom –
a sign that summer has come.
The magical reawakening of
the garden is
helping Colin
regain his
strength.

The children felt that there was magic in the secret garden. All kinds of amazing things happened over the next few months. At first it seemed that green things would never cease pushing their way through the earth, in the grass, in the beds, even through the small gaps in the walls. Then the green things began to show buds, and the buds began to unfurl and show color, every shade of blue, every shade of purple, every tint of crimson.

The seeds Dickon and Mary had planted grew. And the roses! Rising out of the grass, tangled around the sundial, wreathing the tree trunks, and hanging from their branches, climbing up the walls with long garlands falling in cascades – they came alive day by day, hour by hour.

And this was not half of the magic. The fact that he had really once stood on his feet had set Colin thinking tremendously. One day in the garden he called together Dickon, Mary, and Ben Weatherstaff, who had agreed to keep their secret, and made a little speech.

"The magic in this garden has made me stand up and know that I am going to live to be a man. I am going to use the magic to make me strong and well. Now I am going to walk around the garden," Colin announced.

It looked like a parade. Colin was at its head with Dickon on one side and Mary on the other. Ben Weatherstaff walked behind and Dickon's animals trailed after them. Every few yards Colin stopped to rest, and now and then Colin walked a few steps alone.

"I did it! The magic worked!" he cried excitedly. "This is to be the biggest secret of all. No one is to know anything about it until I have grown so strong that I can walk and run like any other boy. I shall come here every day in my chair and I shall be taken back in it. I won't let my father hear about it until I am quite well. Then when he comes back to Misselthwaite I shall just walk into his study and say, 'Here I am: I am like any other boy'."

Colin grew stronger every day. He had made himself believe that he was going to get well, which was really more than half the battle. He and Mary had healthy appetites and ate a lot now, and they were worried that Dr. Craven would no longer believe Colin was ill. So Dickon's mother, Mrs. Sowerby, was let in on the secret, and she sent them milk and bread, which they ate outside. The servants were surprised that after clean plates for weeks the children were now sending back half their meals. But they couldn't help noticing that Mary and Colin were still putting on weight and looking healthier and healthier.

It looked like a parade.

Colin's legs got straighter and stronger every day; the once-sharp chin and hollow cheeks had filled and rounded out. The children all worked together now in the secret garden. Colin was as good at weeding as anyone.

One day Colin dropped his trowel and stretched himself out to his tallest height, throwing his arms open wide. Color glowed in his cheeks. "I'm well. I'm well. I shall find out thousands and thousands of things. I want to shout out something joyful."

Then Colin paused and started looking across the garden at something that had attracted his attention. "Who is coming?" he said quickly. "Who is it?"

A woman entered the garden.

The door in the ivied wall had been pushed gently open and a woman had entered. With the sunlight drifting through the trees and dappling her long blue cloak, she was like a softly colored picture in one of Colin's books.

"It's Mother - that's who it is!" cried Dickon, and he went across the grass at a run.

Colin looked at her for a long time. "Even when I was ill I wanted to see you," he said, "you and Dickon and the secret garden. I'd never wanted to see anyone or anything before."

"Eh! dear lad!" she said, her voice trembling, just as if she might have spoken to Dickon. Colin liked it.

"Are you surprised because I am so well?" he asked.

"Yes, I am!" she said, "but you are so like your mother that you startled me."

"Do you think," said Colin a little awkwardly, "that will make my father like me?"

"For sure, dear lad," she answered, and she gave his shoulder a soft, quick pat. "He must come home and see you."

Then Mrs. Sowerby put both hands on Mary's shoulders and looked over her little face in a motherly fashion. "You've grown too. I think you must be like your mother. Mrs. Medlock said she was a pretty woman."

Mary had not much time to notice her appearance, but she knew that she looked different. She remembered how beautiful her mother had been and was glad that one day she might look like her.

Susan Sowerby went around their garden with them and was shown every bush and tree that had come alive. She had packed a basket which held a real feast, and when the hungry hour came she sat down with them under a tree and watched them devour their food. When she looked at Colin, a quick mist swept over her eyes. "Eh! dear lad! I do believe your own mother's in this very garden. Your father must come back to you – he must!"

Mrs. Sowerby had packed a basket which held a real feast

While the secret garden was blossoming and two children were coming alive with it, Archibald Craven was away traveling. He was a man who for ten years had been full of dark, sad thoughts about his dead wife.

But one night he dreamed that his wife was calling to him.

"Where are you?" he asked.

"In the garden, in the garden!" said the voice.

When he awoke it was a brilliant morning and a letter was waiting for him. It was from Susan Sowerby and it asked him to come home. Mr. Craven decided to return immediately.

When he arrived at the Manor he sent for Mrs. Medlock and asked where Master Colin was. "In the garden, sir," came the reply.

Mr. Craven went outside. He felt as if he were being drawn back to the place he had long forsaken. He knew where the door was.

Then he heard sounds of running feet and muffled laughter. The feet ran faster and faster, they were nearing the garden door – there was quick, strong breathing and a wild outbreak of shouts – the door in the wall was flung wide, a boy burst through it at full speed and, without looking, dashed into his arms.

Mr. Craven clasped the boy to save himself from being knocked over. He held him away to look at him and gasped. He was a tall boy and a handsome one. He was glowing with life, and his running had sent splendid color leaping to his face. But it was his eyes that made Mr. Craven stare.

"Father," the boy said. "I'm Colin. You can't believe it. I scarcely can myself, I'm Colin." He said it all so like a healthy boy – his face flushed, his words tumbling over each other in his eagerness – that Mr. Craven was filled with joy. Colin grasped his

Fall has arrived and the leaves are turning red, gold, and yellow. Everything has come to fruition in the secret garden.

father's arm. "Aren't you glad, Father? I'm going to live forever and ever!"

A boy burst through the door at full speed.

Mr. Craven put his hands on Colin's shoulders and held him. For a moment he could not speak. "Take me into the garden, my boy," he said at last. "And tell me all about it."

And so they led him in. The garden was a wilderness of autumn gold and flaming scarlet. He looked around silently.

"I thought it would all be dead," he said.

"Mary thought so at first," said Colin. "But it came alive."

Then they sat down under a tree, while Colin told his story. "Now," he said when he had finished, "it need not be a secret any more. I shall walk back with you, Father – to the house."

Meanwhile Mrs. Medlock was wondering what was happening. She looked out of the window and gave a cry. Across the lawn came the Master of Misselthwaite. And by his side, with head up in the air, walked as strongly and steadily as any boy in Yorkshire – Master Colin! ✳

Inside the Gardens

AS MARY WANDERS through the gardens of Misselthwaite Manor, she finds formal lawns, an orchard, and kitchen gardens. But then she discovers the private world of a walled garden that has been locked up for ten years.

Kitchen gardens

✱ MANOR GARDENS
This map shows the layout of the gardens of Misselthwaite Manor.

✱ ORDERED WORLD
Misselthwaite Manor, like many big country houses of the time, has large, formal gardens laid out in a regular pattern, with wide lawns and clipped shrubs and hedges.

Walkway

Mary likes to skip around and around a large pool with an old gray fountain in the middle. Plants such as water lilies were often grown in garden pools.

The winding walks protect the closely mown lawns from being trampled on.

Formal Gardens

Mary notices trees cut into "strange shapes." The art of shaping trees is known as topiary.

✳ KITCHEN GARDENS

In the kitchen gardens Ben tends fruit and vegetables for use in the manor house.

✳ SECRET SPLENDOR

The wild beauty of the secret garden contrasts with the order of the formal gardens.

The gardener usually lived in a cottage attached to the kitchen gardens.

Stone seat

Apple and pear trees were grown in the orchard.

The robin guides Mary to the key and the door of the hidden garden.

The key to the garden.

Mary loves to skip along the walkways.

Door covered with ivy

Stone flower urn

Secret Garden

Mary first meets Dickon in a wood just outside the gardens.

The Seasonal Garden

MARY AND DICKON tend the secret garden through the seasons, and watch it grow and flourish. They discover that each season brings its own beauty and has its own tasks to perform.

❋ THE WINTER GARDEN
When Mary first steps inside the secret garden she finds a mysterious gray wilderness of tangled branches and bare stems. With short, cold days, and little sunlight, little grows during winter.

❋ SPRING AWAKENING
Mary and Dickon help bring the garden to life in spring. They clear the soil of weeds to help young shoots grow. After turning over the soil, they plant new flowers and plants.

A springtime scene from the 1993 movie The Secret Garden.

Crocus

❋ SPRING FLOWERS
Though the garden has been left untended, flowers grown from bulbs, such as crocuses and daffodils, survive, because bulbs produce new shoots each year.

Daffodils

❋ SUMMER SECRETS

Like all flower gardens, the secret garden is a riot of color in the warm summer months. Roses – the favorite flower of Colin's mother – spread their blooms everywhere. Other flowers that bloom include poppies and bellflowers.

A beautiful rose garden in full bloom.

❋ FALL GOLD

As leaves turn to Fall colors of gold, red, and brown, the garden is likened to a "temple of gold." It is a time of fulfilment as Colin is reunited with his father and recounts all the magical events that have taken place.

❋ GROWTH AND CHANGE

Just as the garden grows and changes, so does Mary. At the beginning of the story, Mary is bad-tempered, unloved, and thinks only of herself. With the help of Dickon, she tends the garden and brings it to life, and she herself grows in health and happiness and learns the value of true friendship.

Mary

Dickon

❋ MAGIC

The changing garden sparks new life in Mary and she helps Colin develop from a sad, spoiled boy to a happy, healthy young man.

Colin

About the Author

Frances Hodgson Burnett (1849–1924)

FRANCES HODGSON BURNETT was born and brought up in Manchester, England. She was very fond of the family garden, but her family soon moved to the center of Manchester, where there were no gardens – only row upon row of slums. To help escape the ugliness of her surroundings, Burnett began to write stories.

Manchester slums in the 1800s

Little Lord Fauntleroy, 1886

A Little Princess, 1887

✳ SUCCESSFUL DAYS

When Burnett was 16, her family emigrated to the US, and she had several stories published in magazines. Her first children's book, *Little Lord Fauntleroy*, was published in 1886, based on a story she told her own two boys. *A Little Princess* followed soon after in 1887.

✳ A GARDEN OF ROSES

Burnett had never given up her love of gardens; and in 1911, *The Secret Garden* was published – inspired by the old rose garden at Great Maytham Hall in Kent, England, Burnett's second home. The book has since been described as one of the most satisfying children's books ever written.

Great Maytham Hall, Kent